BEAUTIFUL SIGNOR

CYRUS CASSELLS

BEAUTIFUL SIGNOR

 COPPER CANYON PRESS

Hilda Morley's "Mallorcan Love Song" is from *To Hold in My Hand: Selected Poems, 1955–1983* (The Sheep Meadow Press, 1983). Used by permission of Hilda Morley.

Kenneth Rexroth's translation of Chu Shu Chen's "Plaint" is from *100 Poems From the Chinese*. Copyright © 1971 by Kenneth Rexroth. Used by permission of New Directions Publishing Corporation.

Lines from H.D.'s "Hermetic Definition," Copyright © 1969, 1972 by Norman Holmes Pearson. Used by permission of New Directions Publishing Corporation.

Lines from Yeats's "The Phases of the Moon" are from *A Vision*. Used by permission of A.P. Watt Ltd. on behalf of Michael Yeats and by permission of Scribner.

Publication of this book is supported by a grant from the National Endowment for the Arts and a grant from the Lannan Foundation. Additional support to Copper Canyon Press has been provided by the Washington State Arts Commission. Copper Canyon Press is in residence with Centrum at Fort Worden State Park.

Frontispiece: "Portrait of a Young Man," by Galen Garwood.

Library of Congress Cataloging-in-Publication Data

Cassells, Cyrus
Beautiful signor: poems / by Cyrus Cassells
p. cm.
ISBN 1-55659-124-1 (pbk.)
1. Title.
PS3553.A7955B4 1997
811'.54–DC21   97–4699

COPPER CANYON PRESS
P.O. BOX 271, PORT TOWNSEND, WASHINGTON 98368

ACKNOWLEDGMENTS

My deepest gratitude to the Lannan Foundation, to my diligent Italian translator, Damiano Abeni, and to Carolyn Forché, Ken and Peggy McIntosh, Henry Mattison, and Portia Prebys for their great generosity during the writing of this book.

In "Love Poem of the Sicilian Journey" the "city of Persephone" is Agrigento.

In "The Risk-Takers" the lines from the Portuguese are my own translation of words from the song "Guitar," adapted from the *fado* poets, and performed by the popular Portuguese group Madredeus.

"Dante Comes to the Troubadour's Defense" is dedicated to Carmela Merola.

Special thanks to Aaron Shurin for allowing me to use the last words of his moving essay, "Some Haunting," in "Love Poem with the Wind of Calvary." The book's title was inspired by the phrase "the beautiful clustering Signor" from his poem "Portal."

"The Dream of the Minoan Palace of Knossos" is dedicated to the memory of a gallant scholar, John Boswell.

In "Amalgam" the incident alluded to occurred in Bergen-Belsen, and is recounted in Shirley Kaufman's poem "By the Rivers."

Grateful acknowledgment is made to the editors of the following journals and anthologies in which these poems first appeared (some in earlier versions): *The Bellingham Review*, *The Crab Orchard Review*, *The English Digest of Tunisia*, *Eros in Boystown* (Crown Publishers), *The James White Review*, *Pivot*, *Provincetown Arts*, *The Stonybrook Journal*, and *Things Shaped in Passing: More "Poets for Life" Writing from the* AIDS *Pandemic* (Persea Books).

CONTENTS

MALLORCAN LOVE SONG

I know why for a week
I have not slept more than half the night,
awake with the small moon
                            & with every
bird-cry,
            every shift of light:
                        I have
this burden on me which will not let me sleep

I have the sweet
pain, the *douce douleur* the troubadours
speak of
           Ease me
                  I am bruised with
the weight of the burden
                       Here where they sang,
the *lourd fardeau* is upon me
                          Like them, I come to you
saying: you have given me this burden
                            Lift it
with your touch

— HILDA MORLEY

PLAINT

Spring flowers, autumn moons,
Water lilies still carry
Away my heart like a lost
Boat. As long as I am flesh
And bone I will never find
Rest. There will never come a
Time when I will be able
To resist my emotions.

– CHU SHU CHEN

BEAUTIFUL SIGNOR

GUITAR

At a peace-granting, indigo hour,
the Andorran moon
blanches,
through the parted shutters,
your spatulate fingers, the feminine
shape of the guitar.
Though you're guardless,
enmeshed in dreams,
I'm already imagining
fresh chords.

When I tongue your lids
at cockcrow,
I'll confide:
in a paramount dream,
before meeting,
I'm cross-my-heart sure I heard
your questing, phenomenal guitar,
our blended voices,
as through a zephyr in a garden's
sorcery,
a deep fragrance precedes
a treasurable flower,
sometimes a peerless
harmony is fashioned
before it's lived –

We come from families
of dauntless travelers
and poets.

We wander the hallowing Pyrenees,
and the hem of an ancient,
venerable sea,
under parasol pines,
or a piquant blue zenith,
for there's always
a commanding view, a new
facet of love
to ponder –

We're troubadours
because we've learned
from the burrs of plague and war:
life on earth is
brief, keen, incendiary –

Periwinkles, yarrow,
a barefoot sibyl
unriddling her Romeo's
safeguarded palm,
gloves of moonlight,
the guitar's compliance,

today these will become
our song.

I

THE MAGICIAN-MADE TREE

And the Swiss signora's cordial horses
come to water at my serenade.
I open teal shutters to a swatch
of Tuscan hills, roofs, swallows,
and let the songs and syllables rain,
hi-lili, hi-lo,
upon the grove of impeccable bamboo,
upon the Buddha-still, soothing field
where they drink.

They seem fond
of my singing,
with its thin, fraying selvage
of sorrow for what's lost,
irretrievable –
these summerstruck, beneficent, sipping mares.
They have patience:
your provender to me,
as I clasp your language,
culling words
for what might give you balm –

Once in a placid dream,
I lay in merciful grass,
and a lissome colt
curled at my chest,
as if to suckle there –
as you did,
opening my muslin shirt

in the midnight cool
of the field beside the Villa Flury:

I have no milk, only tenderness.

II. THE MAGICIAN-MADE TREE

At first taste, I wrote:
the keen trace of your kiss
is the cool memory
of a fig's sweetness
in September heat.

But that was just metaphor,
dreaming –

Today we embraced under a branch
in mummyish Linari;
all the terraced hills
with their ready olives, grapes,
seemed to rise around us,
as you stopped and gestured to
the magician-made tree.

Then you plucked its pure manna,
and fed me amid kisses.

For a roiling week I've wanted only
your champion flesh under trees,
glorybound clouds –
your hushing hand
nimbly unlatching
my spirit cache of small things:
the glitter of the Arno
at wolf's hour,
a monk's pert whistle,
market lemons, intrepid
shards of majolica, a blind man
tapping his cane
under a sky of shooting stars:
they beat inside me
these keepsakes,
like finches
in a Franciscan cloister;
on the road from Fiesole
to Castel di Poggio,
I'd let you treasure them,
uncaged –

Can you imagine ambling,
giddy in the green thrall
of Gulliver-tall cypresses?

Puissant pines, a cat
the color of champagne
for our ally.

Come with me.

Holy of holies, pleasure flecked
with weeping
for joy, for joy: our cries
caught in the soughing trees,
our cries seized
by a gossiping jay:
clement thighs, hips, fingertips, clement
kiss of Demerara rum.
When you looked into my eyes, my face,
on the deer path, saying
my beard is not a hunter's beard,
did you know this would happen?:

hooves,
the splendid voyeurism of the buck,
snorting, pawing the earth beside us –
it only wants to feel
what we feel –
and your blissful lips,
your breath at my nipples.

V. NEW SONG OF SOLOMON

Look how we're wedded –
jubilant, unchecked.
The armoire mirror
is our witness:
this is a new Song of Solomon
we're fashioning;
in Tuscan niches
where our bed is green
or trophy-bright,
in shuttered
Florentine and Roman rooms,
your body has become
my refuge and intoxicant.

You've given me
rosemary, trumpet lilies, musk, God
in the hours of languor.
You've given me
calamus and cinnamon,
your hand's acumen.

I want the crush of your pelvis,
your outlaw kiss.
I want your inmost wonder,
your fierce mouth
here. And here.

VI. THE RIVER GOD

On a Sabbath walk, we learn
each of our first loves
died in our youth.
We stray off the road;
in the simmering dusk,
in the coppice's wild quiet,
our discomfiting clothes
scattering – a little flurry
in the lizard kingdom –
your skin in a matchless
garment of shadow,
evocative of a statue
in a spare museum room:
Michelangelo's *Model of a River God.*

Like us, the Renaissance genius puzzled
why rustic deities and lovers
sally into love, arrayed
only in flesh, bruisable flesh,
if the tournament's end is always
willowy mourning:

against the undertow,
your body, siphoned for a while
of sorrow –
will I ever love you more
than in this place
where voices of reproach
can't reach us,

all the meshes of dismay –
your irrepressible cry
navigating the insurgent thighs
Buonarroti bends
to fashion out of clay.

I can say it now,
what his hands meant:
a shamefaced pleasure.
I was small;
he was in charge
of me,
and his peacock name
was the name of this sumptuous
gondolier's city
of your birth:

by some justice,
balanced, inspiriting,
now life has given me
a Venetian man.

What was it like
to grow up in Venice?

Always the feeling of water
and protective stone –

If I'm unchecked rain, a gale
on your family balcony,
it's because
your *joie de vivre* fingers,
the glass-green canals,
the filigree
and gold-leaf luxury
release me;

it's because
suddenly I hear
my father recalling,
after long amnesia,
a belt around his throat,
baleful hands hauling him
into an alley –
till we breathe together,
boys of the same age,
father and son,
beleaguered,
mirrored in our wounding;

it's because
I have a choice
to emerge from this maze,
unalarmed,
unmolested,
my garnered power to select
intact –
to love this time
with all my being.

VIII. THE BLUE TULIP

Out of voicelessness, deep
sanctity,
comes this blue tulip;
from boyhood, I've
blessed it,
dreamed it into bloom.
I don't know why,
or where:
always in sleep,
the hill with its coverlet
of asters,
where I lay me down
in fathomless peace,
and then the pliant
garden below
unmapped mountains –

For years I've felt
no need
to share the marvel.
But now,
from a locketed,
paradisiacal place,
like a proffering god,
for you,
I'll make the lustrous,
azure petals
mortal, my love,
visible at last
in the human world.

IX. THE IRIS

Slender iris,
from earliest memory,
I've crowned you,
praised you above
all the other delicate
constituents of the garden.
Like you, my love's
fostered by the sun,
his soul,
a surefire purple,
with an easeful flame,
a chasuble of genteel
saffron –
so as he brings you,
felicitous, revered
bloom,
my eyes passing
from delight
to delight,
I'm transported again:
childtime
in the unerring garden
beside the stalks.

X. THE BARGAIN

In the transatlantic fury
when I feared
I might not survive
to see Florence,
clutching an elfin
Love Sonnets of Shakespeare,
I implored:
*Lord, let me live
long enough to dare
a love poem* –

In time, of course, the skies
stopped glowering.
And in the Tuscan summer's imperial
segue into autumn,
poetry burgeoned –

It's not only the active grace,
the glory between us:
these praise songs spring
from a holy bargain,
from my deepest desire
to live.

THE FOOL, THE FOREIGNER

I. THE GREEN PUZZLE

I open the door:
Rome with its countless fountains –

My new language
swirls in from the street,
keen and captivating –

At a café table,
enchanting industry:
children fingering
intriguing puzzle pieces;

in the drowsy
siesta hours,
what will their persistence
reveal?
Trees?
A transporting sea?
And what will the assembled
greenness mean
to their spirits?

II. THE INTERRUPTION

Today while learning *tiglio*
for the linden,
I feel your voice,
lulling, summery,
pass through my very being,

so that I have to excuse myself
from the garrulous classroom:

crazy troubadour, you think
someone feels our lovemaking
in heaven!

From the lavatory, I watch
slanted light on a terrace –
like the light
on the ermine and pearls
of Vermeer's women –
as a towhee
reaches the sill –

Rampant tears:
to be so human,
to be so graced
with the rose-holding hope
of the unperturbed
fool in the tarot,
as he steps off a promontory;

perhaps this boot-shaped land
will be my net:

here goes, here goes.

QUARTET

I. LOVE POEM OF THE UMBRIAN NIGHT

It happens, love looms
again in your lifetime.
Sweet ambush, sweet
ferocity and surprise –

Ecstasy:
under the Pleiades,
the detectable Dippers, the path
flooded with fireflies,
the heartfilled dark
a passe-partout,
a dance hall,
rife with galaxies.
Dream the measureless music.
Take this
reckless, imagined rose –

See how your shadow
links with mine;
on moonlit grass now,
the pet lamb
and the pampered dog,
heedless,
hushed as statuary –

How it beats,
your heart that was once
directionless.
And in this precinct

of showy stars,
the serene, upreaching cypress
is our lauded lord,
our Caesar.

II. THE TRAMPOLINE

Now our souls' clues billow
like dervishes' skirts, imagine –
getaway-wild, unbridled,
unignorable.
And the eyes
of our hearts are open,
open to the zones of joy.
Gadabouts,
under our lids,
we leap and leap,
as if we might never
touch the trampoline again.

III. THE GRAIL

Now that we're freed,
unbossed,
unsullied
by a shame without end,
I see:

without uplifting clarity,
love is crippling:
the flash of an Excalibur,
or a bridge
to bitterness, idolatry;

how quick we are to worship
what's outside our skin,
never gleaning
our own radiance –

The Romulus and Remus
of wisdom and desire,
valiant, inseparable,
love, love,
that's what our Grail is.

IV. LOVE AND HUMAN FRAILTY

Happiness?

It's not as if we can't see
the legless Christ
in the piazza;
his farrago of shirts,
his filthy wagon,
his eyes of a castaway,
are all too clear;

it's just that suddenly
his shrillness and squalor,
our exuberance,
seem at last
one single movement
in the allotted
symphony of the shareable day –

In the life we fashion,
let's resist the temptation
to be Oxford dons about
what we might not be able
to share.

Take my apparent ramparts,
the moat and frangible heart:

perhaps my frailties will have
some meaning for you.

TUNISIAN DIARY

Incomparable leisure:
musk
at your pulse;

mist
on the pendant lemons,
full,
then fading sun –

In the trellised garden, a deft,
caressing wind.

And suddenly the day's end
is prodigal
with jasmine.

*

In a ghostly street,
from an undetectable
window,
pour drums and a chorus
of Arab children;

for a long while
you listen,
rapt, immobile –

Now my heart is full of you
in the white street.

*

Near the surf,
at noon,
the muezzin's call
to prayer
cleanses us
as surely as the sea's
apron of utter turquoise.

*

After love, it's soothing
to let you sleep,
to stroll unvexed
into the village,
with only tattered
Arabic and French,
to sip sweet tea
beside musing lingerers
puffing serpentine pipes,
to slip into perfumed
or acrid streets,
indistinguishable from Arab men.

*

At times it's true:
I feel one
with the unpersuadable
lion's roar –

But in Carthage,
before mosaics
clarified by rain,
in the remnants
of a Roman villa,
I'm dulcet, immaculate
as truce,
when you call me *dove*.

LOVE POEM OF THE SICILIAN JOURNEY

Blessed passenger,
on this embraceable journey,
don't be shy:
scale the volcano,
linger at the sensuous fountain.

*

For my birthday,
I've the white tulips
orphaned by a drowsy Lothario
whose station was Messina,

our joyous, transiting brocade
of jew's-harp and whistle,
voice and guitar.

*

Where venturing boats,
inching starfish prosper,
so coruscating,
the sea is never destitute;

now the nets are bullioned
with writhing fish:
a bobbing countinghouse.

*

Out of the shower, singing
fly to my side,
fly to my side,

singing
savor me as you would
the first taste
of the winepress,
the wedding cup.

*

When you wake me in the grotto
with doctoring lips
and flesh,
all sienna-skinned
freedom and skill,
it's the dazzling
sea trace, the salt
droplets from your bracing swim
that I savor.

*

At a train stop,
we're enchanted witnesses
to the gleeful man
who strikes,
on an eroding plinth,
an uproarious
statue's pose,
as the stationmaster
frowns.

*

On a weatherworn parapet,
this peregrine soul:

a gull,
indolent between heaven and earth.

*

In the arresting
amphitheater at Siracusa,
the actors are preparing
Prometheus Bound:
charming, make-believe cypresses,
long robes in the midday sun.

*

Suddenly, an auburn-haired boy
skipping in an alleyway,
brisk beneath
the slant of a volcano.

*

And when it's time to dream,
we let them dangle
from the headboard,
our crusader puppets –
here come the infidels! –
our champions;

they evoke the wild pink
lilies we picked
one dusk, and placed
in a bedside vase;

far into the night,
under lodestars,
their enlivening scent,
their fetching, ingratiating aegis.

*

Though it's verdant spring,
in the soul of
the wizened lacemaker
as she unwraps her work,
it's stubbornly February:

a presiding music
of euphoric almond blossoms.

*

In winter we prized
Chinese poetry:
"the city is full
of flying pear flowers";

now, pears gleaming
on an heirloom plate,
bell notes beside our bed,
my "bodhisattva mouth."

*

How I love our holiday bed:
our April nakedness, our shares
of Sicilian almond milk and cake,
our Easter words
and exultant whispers
forever pointing us away
from misery –
camerados whose linked
spirits are an archway
to a fairground,
a festival.

How I love this equipoise,
this immersion:
two men,
untrammeled, at peace.

Now I know
it's possible on earth:
to dispense with the bridle
of *"you and I,"*
to grow
boundaryless, boundaryless:

ruby holding the red
of sunrise,
pond cradling the Milky Way.

*

Poppies in the trainyard,
on the visible hills, poppies
in the city of Persephone,

and everywhere the bold
sultan's purple of bougainvillea,
the fanfare of broom,

everywhere May meadows
full of sudden pillows;
over our truant heads, a harried
canopy of swallows,

on this island
of conquest and catastrophes,
this supple island –

With a frank and courteous chamois,
you swab your outburst
from my palm,

and my heart is an unfailing
Icarus ascending.

THE RISK-TAKERS

Take me anywhere, anywhere;
I walk into you,
Doge – Venice –
you are my whole estate...

– H.D., *Hermetic Definition*

I.

The journey begins here:
time and again, time and again,
grace me
with a love deluxe,
the attendant hands
of a page-turner.
Let the absolving city
shore us, a brimful
garden of delights.
Let rest-in-peace popes
and living kings
of flummery
grant us passage,
usher us, unmussed, beyond
ravishing, tenacious
realms of stone,
fearsome traffic –

Carry my spirit,
as a peasant conveys,
good-natured arms
akimbo,

a profusion of flowers
on her head –
her poise
miraculous, startling
in the Roman street,
equal to the weight
of her bright,
capacious bundle –

When you walk
openshirted, alone,
by the ambered current,
the riverbank trees,
carry my spirit.

II.

What the Sufis, the headlong
troubadours acclaimed,
what the dervishes danced toward –
the worthy risk,
the wild-hearted gift,
scintilla of heaven –
you are, you are,
beautiful Signor.

Like the regnant moon,
or a tantalized gull,
and the heartened sea reaching up
with never-forlorn
hands of foam,
we haunt,
we ennoble each other.

And no threat from stringent
mandarins of order,
no harsh wind,
no fiat can extinguish
the passion in my soul.

In the Maltese ruins
of Hagar Qim,
"the Stones of Adoration,"
or on a golden belvedere above
a river's green braid,
like a stellar galleon,
like a rose whose scent

is passage to a new Valhalla,
you are, you are,
beautiful Signor.

III.

Human dawn,
over the buffeting,
entangling earth,
I searched and searched for you,
and only when I stilled
my desperate longing,
did you appear:
integrity's crowning triumph –

If I whirl
in lavish ecstasy,
if I weep
in your steadying arms,
beautiful Signor,
it's to remind me:
you were once a faraway sea –

And now, in a prodigious dream,
God leans down –
God the Kindling Fire,
God the Pollen,
God the Catapulting Joy –
to reveal:

even my downfalls,
my cat's cradle compromises,
even my abysses,
were my path to you.

IV.

And the abeyance,
the waiting that felt lifelong,
the adversarial,
the ungiving –
they're vanquished;
the suffering of lovers
we left behind,
our selfsame suffering,
we take it off,
like a tattered shirt.
Clamorous streets,
passersby who seemed so many
spellbound ants –
we approach them
with compassion,
newfound, unending –
the streets a little
hawkish still,
and rollicking,
but riskable now,
the cities,
once daunting,
supercilious,
become scattered
necklaces seen from the air.

v.

We've known *maybe yes, maybe no*,
we've weathered *wait and see*;
we've known love's
mummy wrappings,
its duncecap desires,
its dispiriting shipwrecks
and exquisite throes.

Suddenly we're apt,
on the go: entrancing
spaghetti straps,
Sardinian candies,
the rushing Po,
piano notes in a sleepy
alleyway of Lucca;

in Gubbio,
on a day dull as porridge,
a parachutist plummets
into a field before us,
beside an ancient amphitheater:

in a world always
at loggerheads,
authentic love seems
that comet's-tail festive.

VI.

Amid scattered
bedclothes, dawn-lit,
empty bottles, you sing
at my awakening,
notes like delicate
bird steps
over my body,
until the hour passes,
and your songs fade,
beautiful Signor,
into the first sounds
of Roman streets:
the earliest tram,
and the humming of a hardy
fruit vendor –

Lift from me the armor
born of moments
full of sting,
when my daft, abraded heart
felt no one's beloved.
Fill me as you fill
the black, slender prayer
of your clarinet.
Give me your trustworthy strings
and I'll learn to sing,
after Lisbon's *fado* poets:

when I die,
let my coffin be
a bit bizarre,
heart-shaped,
or in the shape of a guitar.

VII.

If you've sung to me before,
sing to me again,
but with an oarsman's brio,
row us to a kingdom,
a reconciling shore,
where we might become
bold and housebroken,
bachelor and cornered groom
in the same breath –

And when you wrest some small
closure from the guitar,
like the last flourishing
vestiges of rain,
I want my upraised
soul to be
your Aladdin's carpet,
my flesh
your spinning wheel to attain
a straw-into-gold glory,
my hips
your renegade throne,
your resting place –

In welling trust,
we're traveling:
from station
to elating station,

paint my heart the red,
paint my heart the red,
paint my heart the red
of a red-winged blackbird.

VIII.

Now children appear
on petting ponies,
in undisguised delight,
and shy, enthralling brides step
gingerly through the summer grasses.
What are you waiting for?
If the curt, the quotidian
drains you,
reach for me
in the flower-covered world,
amid the little salvos
of June roses.
Be my jewelry,
be my panoply and joy.
Let my limbs
be the antidote,
till you reach beyond
the slapdash,
to the showstopping,
the nonpareil,
like a memory of Maria Callas
caressing the glittering,
topmost chandeliers,
rending all
the witnessing hearts –

Muster your faith
and ecstasy,
never fail to praise
the mast-high,

the pinnacle,
what might be achieved:
the probity of La Callas.

IX.

A return to awe, a deeper
reverence for the flesh,
that's what the cadenced days
have given us.
In the Metro, everywhere
praiseworthy eyes:
brook brown,
cogent blue, and ardent,
unfettered green,
my favorite –

As long as I'm flesh
and bone,
I'll never be done
with your agile strength,
the mainstay
of your animated face, your eyes'
ravishing persuasion –

A small earthquake
in a Roman theater,
and the landscape,
and the resolute protagonists
keep on flowing above
the spilling popcorn,
the viewers' puzzlement –

But what was that look
you gave me,
in the middle of the tremor?
Though I try to limn its
death-will-not-part-us vigor,

as we exit the moviehouse,
man who has become my well,
I fail magnificently,
I fail.

x.

As an acolyte in assiduous prayer
craves God's
galvanizing face,
so I crave your soulstuff,
your quintessential core.

How brave of you
to let me peer into your
one-in-a-million spirit,
beautiful Signor,
beyond shield and breastplate
to boyhood
places of wounding.

And now I bare, in turn,
precincts beneath my lids
that cry out
for redemption
or demolition,
where the bullying world
reigns, a slumlord –

Of all creatures,
my ally,
my accomplice in folly,
let me be grasped
and recognized by you.

All night
this lovers' engine,

this Pegasus:
seeing and being seen,
seeing and being seen.

XI.

And I find in you
the ochre and gold,
the lustrous, silvery green
of the olive fields above Assisi.
And I find in you
the ineffable pink
of the renowned saint's
open palms,
the white, like fountain foam,
of an unabashed
almond in bloom,
find in you
the sky with a linnet-blue
of our Brother Wind's scapular:

of this spectrumed love,
always remember
there is an allaying portion left
for the Sister Larks,
the beggar's makeshift bowl –

Sometimes this utmost praise
braves the world
barefoot, conversant with stones
and seraphim:
oh here is a caress,
an empathy to quell
the prowling wolf,
a calm of bundled arrows, doves...

XII.

You untie two coppery horses
and coax me:
but I don't know how to ride!

Yet, in time,
I let my unease
evanesce,
as on sand we rush past
a roll call of towering palms,
let the mane and sweat and sinew
smash the saturnine, sallow boat
anchored inside me –

In China looms a gate
a poet in a pipe dream named
"there is another cave of heaven":

on a mare,
gentle as the Nazarene,
with a scintillant moon
enthroned above foam,
I feel my brimming
spirit on a dare
pass through that gate,
pass through.

XIII.

Your soul is a fountainspray,
an incense,
beautiful Signor,
deranging my material noons,
my roguish nights –

When the shadows become runnels,
the pine and cypress shadows,
and the Colosseum is a vessel
of late light,
I take the memory
of your hands,
the bell notes
of your name,
the musk of you
with me as I walk
around the ruin,
its grandeur
inseparable from cruelties   .
and sagas –

Companion of the Roman summer,
chance-taker, let me cherish
your many avatars,
your risks and alleluias,
even the thrown-to-the-lions
deaths you've endured,

for already you seem adamant,
timeless as these stones;
for already I've glimpsed
in increments,
your never-ending soul.

XIV.

It can't be winnowed from the world,
this heart-marauding
frenzy to be linked,
this passion,
though, over and over,
the round earth's infinite wardens
have tried:
we're immersed in trenchant time
and yearning flesh –

As an old, dreamworn woman
weaves fresh forget-me-nots
into her hair,
gun-gray, yet lush,
let the unacclaimed days
subsume us.
Open yourself
away from the slipshod,
the sullen,
away from the indeterminate,
friend in the experiment.
Walk with me in the world's
crucible heat and promise.
Make this love possible,
as all things are possible.

LOVE POEM OF THE ROMAN DAYS

I. THE AUSTRIAN COAT

Beautiful Signor,
from my casement beside
the basilica,
the market's bedlam, lifted
from morning reverie,
I watch you,
walking in your Austrian coat,
like no other man –
with your coat,
you sheltered me
from the brigand tempest,
the noonday hail,
with your coat,
you made a blanket,
chivalrous, impromptu,
in the stirring meadow –
you whom the corner boys,
the stray cats cotton to,
the scruffy cobbler reveres.

I love the sound
of your steps in my stairwell,
sure-footed, yet
pizzicato,
implausibly delicate,
in my doorframe again,
the feel of applaudable,
pine-colored cloth.

II. THE VIEW FROM VIA SANNIO

Sunday: the market's still, the street,
gossipless and serene.
Above the basilica,
the Roman sky blooms,
as never before,
and I must wake you,
give you this view,
garnet, roseate, gill-blue –
A gull delights
in San Giovanni's façade,
the pale row of mystics,
passing from crown to crown –

We love the morning man,
saint of the neglected,
neighbor blessing the esplanade
with glinting scraps,
morsels for the gruff, masterless cats
ensconced by the ancient wall –
hands full, coat pockets
fecund with coins,
to affirm we are all
bishops and kings,
beggars and stewards –

For us in our ardor,
there's only one city,
one sill.

III. THE OPERA LOVER'S APPRENTICE

Is it your will,
lovemaker, connoisseur,
always porous with swigs
of opera,
that each time
along the Tiber I approach
the looming
Castel Sant'Angelo,
I wince,
reliving
Tosca's impassioned leap?

IV. ROMAN DISGUISES

In masked and merry Rome,
on Fat Tuesday, whom will you be,
my love, and what?
We're sworn to secrecy.
At the costumer's,
I linger at Methuselah,
the moon and accompanying stars,
then assume
the laurel crown,
the illustrious red robes
of Dante – like a rabbit
in preening tie and tails –

Amid the revelry's tussle,
you're not hard to detect:
your soul's so luminous;
it's you, it's you beside
the Elizabethan queen,
the sullen sultan –

After the ephemeral blaze
of a masked ball,
there's a bold
veil of silk, a kiss
through a corsair's sleeve;
there's the unbridled vignette
embedded in the whisper:
no, keep the mask on.

V. SONG OF ROMAN SUN

Sun on the plane trees,
the bride's taffeta,
sun on the grizzled walls;
the city's a god sprayed
with graffiti –

Brief shower: the windblown
cassocks of priests,
the wet, expressive hands
of a garlic seller,
a sudden chaos of umbrellas,
then a man whose brimming eyes
exactly match
the azure of his umbrella –

Not long ago
it was heady Carnival.
Scuffed revelers' confetti,
already the rain, the winter's
thrownaway:
sun on the stone
lion's mane above the door,
the stone Artemis,
the stone mermaid,
sun on the butcher-blessed
rosemary –

Under a showstopping
bough's wizardry,
a live-a-little bed
of cool clover;

in the emboldening city
where I embrace you,
a city renewed by rain,
I want to be to you
what the masterly afternoon is
to the upraised,
suddenly vivacious cherries.

Now the whine
of irksome gypsies, the crisp
humility of nuns.
Spring shakes the hodgepodge city
like a shout.
I'm not sure if you can hear me,
love; there's a baby's
powerhouse bawl,
a fountain's plash, the earnest
plea of a tourist:
how do you cross the street? –

A ragwoman yawns
from her jerry-built bed
of morning papers –

There's no metropolis
with more worlds
than this one; every inch
occupied, embellished,
pulsing with point of view:
the earth catacombed, the ceilings
boisterous with wings –

Here's the knife grinder
in another piazza:
I never knew
his business was mobile! –

And your voice,
flecked with tenderness
on the public phone,
avid to reach me,
your voice
in a splendid, clamorous city:
Lord,
let me hear it.

VII. ISABELLA'S TREE

In the courtyard, Isabella's apricot,
spurred by the rain,
goaded by the sun,
iterates its delicate
whiteness, its unabashed
languor under a living
arabesque of swallows –

Isabella's in love:
my friend Peter trekked to Rome,
thinking only to escape
New England winter;
now they're exuberant,
coupled –

Cupid, general
of hot desire,
don't let this joy
evanesce, this glorious March
go unmonumented –

When Peter's far away,
will Isabella's faith surmount
the chilly miles?

Is *besotted*
the word she wants,
now that the once blasé courtyard
is lambent with blossoms,

and the spirited wisteria burgeons,
dauphin into king,
dauphin into king.

VIII. SONG OF ROMAN SPRING

April: spry wind
embellishes our tranquil walks
in the Villa Torlonia,
the Villa Pamphili;
I'm listening to you:
voice and heartbeat,
whisper and pulse.
We've cheered
passion's appearance,
the brisk match-burst of a cardinal
veering from boxwood,
but now I want to praise
steadiness, contentment,
like the daisies' affable beauty beside
the moonlit columns –

With a blithe, mercurial palette,
you improvised
a border of daisies
for my door;

now each day I enter
a realm of daisies.
And like the flower
this quickening season,
you are everywhere:
salient,
sheer gold at the center.

IX. ETRUSCAN SHOWER

Deep in Etruscan earth, we laugh
at erotic revelers
enlivening a buried tomb
in Tarquinia.
Later, from a seaside niche,
we notice,
above a faraway crest
of wildflowers,
another couple,
like a hectic, immoderate
Adam and Eve –
the headland supernal,
trenchant between us –
till harridan clouds
send us scurrying
back to the lot,
where the laggard day acquires
sterner colors –
Prussian blue, bruise blue, pewter –
brisk artillery, a fusillade
of drumbeats, and woven
into the roar, a rumor
of Etruscan flutes,
castanets;
now the drenched car
encloses us
like a tomb –

We roll down a window,
after the percussive shower.
Coolness on our throats
and nipples.
Prehensile vines,
flamelike flowers,
the field still tempestuous
and swaying.

I want this sacredness to stay:
the bronze and rouge
of the summer solstice,
the excavated city,
poppy-lit, fantastic, freaked
with the embers of spring.
And the sage, convivial
butterfly that seemed
a fellow celebrant
in the democracy of awe,
I want its genial hovering
near us still –

In your newborn summer sleep,
I'll be disguised
as the ruins of Ostia:
bring to benevolent light
whatever begs
to be unearthed;
goblets, coins, splendid
Neptune mosaics;
in your living hands now,
beauty no longer immured,
glory no longer hampered –
Cherish these intact stones
which are my flesh.
Idle here,
luxuriate;
wend through me for hours.

XI. WE DON THE MASKS OF HADRIAN AND ANTINOUS

AT THE VILLA ADRIANA

red lily wide open
under the sun's warm coin

fireworks imprisoned
in a glance

extravagant noonday bells

bold tor of shoulder
where the falcon rests

tender and vernal nude

suicide at the first
breath print of age

body lifted
out of taciturn silt

all faces becoming your face

love, love, no need to look,
distinguish,
no need to count anymore

all faces alchemized,
obliterated

all faces becoming
one trumpeted face

XII. SLEEPLESS NIGHT

If the Roman night impinges
with its active
citizens of marble,
its heavy cowl
of history, humidity,
let me nestle
my sleepless head
to your chest,
the plush, agreeable fan
of dark hair,
let me listen intently –
as when I sauntered
through the sibyl's cave
at Cuma,
rife with soundholes;

in reverie,
let me acquire
a seer's power
to discern,
deep within you,
your aunt's sovereign,
resuscitating soprano,
a derelict radio jingle,
an innermost psalm
to the sea:

no smoking tripod,
but the wavecrest mystery
of a single life,
the manifold voices
resounding, resounding…

An accordion embroiders the morning
with sweet thread,
so we hurry to the sill,
and let the unexpected hush
the hawkers' cries,
the fishmonger's lungs,
the knife grinder's sibilant labor.

A soul-sharing girl
sings from an open window,
and suddenly they're here:
the invigorating notes
that halt the clockwork broom,
that snuff the hoary argument,
like a deep kiss –
the frenetic city
winning once more,
emollient in its pell-mell beauty:

on the fourth floor, a stout
man in a bathrobe
harmonizes,
and in the courtyard, the disheveled maid
grown ebullient as a lark...
and now you lift
from the careworn cot
the no-longer-dreaming guitar:

Troubadours, your song restores me,
leads me to the calmest country;

you are the polestar
and the waterborne wish,
the Tiber's cool tunic:
the shimmer and the depth,
the shimmer and the depth.

GHOSTS

A voice,
the quick snick of a stone;
when I lean from a sill,
no one's there.
Madame Mannant says a woman
haunts this hilltop;
so we bloom into detectives
who trace Madame's phantom,
still pining for her troubadour,
whose fillip of *alba, alba,*
wounds the air
whenever sunup
bids him away from her bower.

Lily among thorns,
now I am as attuned,
as attentive to you
as to the moon's
telltale phases,
to Venus ascending,
to Venus going down,
to Venus hidden by the earth.

And this is the tale we shape,
the ballad:
amid lush vines and fennel,
lavender, a siege
of lavender,

she waits –
fisher king, my breasts,
my body,
would be the lake
where your wound is eased,
the lovingkindness –
never learning
a tempest hurled him
from his roan –

In eleven centuries,
ash and clamor,
how the tales accrete,
like dark casks cradling
the many years of wine –

All night burnishing
the spindrift, the haunting, the horse
in the heckling storm,
till the ghosts become
ourselves –

A cock crows,
tattered chanticleer,
but we can't hear:
alba, alba;
we've fallen asleep.

DANTE COMES TO
THE TROUBADOUR'S DEFENSE

When we walk together
in the Pyrenees,
where the unflagging
patriarchs are playing ball,
or on the promontory
as the moon soars
with a cheerful retinue
of belled cows,
I want to sing:
in autumn fields,
in tenantless dells,
love seized me –

True, like a man or woman spied
at rare intervals,
you're vaunted, unalloyed
in praise songs:
look, look,
now your arms are gold,
and at your imbuing touch,
a lamp eases on:

so the poet's endowed,
like Dante in ghastly realms,
with love's gleam and ammunition –

I hear a callow,
incredulous student:

no woman like Beatrice
could possibly exist!

Beatrice exists.

FROM THE THEATER OF WINE

Suddenly we're sons of Noah,
in biblical robes,
wielding showy censers
to start with pomp
a Rosh Hashanah preschool pageant.
When the whirling incense
clears from the open courtyard
of the old kabbala school,
and the small children have quelled
their raucous coughing,
barrels of ripeness are brought in,
and tin pans,
brimming with the vineyards' glory.
Soon Noah's mightily confused,
mock intoxicated...

As you take a jesterly bow,
autumn sun glistens in the auburn
of your Old Testament wig.
And spry Noah is filling
the lush, tousled lap
of his lavish beard
with grapes.
And the barefoot children are learning
a fruit-breathed laughter,
as they stamp and savor the labor
in the jubilant lesson of wine.

LOVE POEM OF THE PYRENEES

In the hush after coupling,
calm's pearled cotillion,
we listen as if,
at an iridescent hour,
the Pyrenees themselves
could sing –

How simply it crests within us,
this heaven-in-the-other,
human, yet unsurpassed.
On this long night
of lilac and tobacco,
we praise its sweetness,
knowing the spiritless squander it
as maquillage,
or a pitiless scepter
in a palace of incest –

Find the bell pull,
bring down the morning star
to allay us:
sex is a troubadour's pulse,
a song:

bivouac of twilight,
bridge of mountain dawn.

THE CALYCANTHUS FLOWERS

Now the mountains come close
with their hint
of Switzerland, their fresh
bridles of snow.
Come to my balcony,
share with me this utmost
healing majesty:
gloom-banishing boats,
the cormorant's motion –

No need to speak:
these flowers in a jar,
pale as tallow –
I know they mean
forgiveness:

Calycanthus.

Make us one
with the daymoon, the grotto,
the pillars of cypress.

Make us one
with the panorama.

Calycanthus, Calycanthus.

Touch me,

make me porous
with an indispensable
midwinter bloom,
and a fragrance of soul
to match.

LOVE POEM WITH THE WIND OF CALVARY

— ROSSO FIORENTINO'S
Deposition From the Cross

My love, all season I've stared
at Rosso Fiorentino's pallid
savior and son,
the unstinting arms, the windswept
garments of his followers,
as they clasp
the cherished body become
inert as a marionette –
green limbs, green limbs –
the Renaissance painter's palette
harrowing, immediate,
his altarpiece suffused
with helplessness,
as if this happened here today:

the jolting, cold ladders
of mourning,
Mary, pierced to the quick –
who in his hubris would unmake
a woman's labor? –
and the Magdalen, a carmine
flare at the base of the cross,
a carmine pleading:
no, not this –

Unbearable knowledge, the desolating
wind in the hospice:

now the disease has seeped
through the blood/brain barrier,
and our friend murmuring,
plague-wracked, gallant,
jettisoned from youth:
I am not disease only;
hold me as you would hold
the body of Christ –

Love, love, here are my lids,
fragile as leafdrift,
my flesh, mortal
to the infinite power;
against Time's ruffian wind,
for all our days remaining,
hold me as you would hold
the body of Christ –

Tell the lightning-struck,
inconsolable apostle
turning away
from his sapless king
in lush tears,
in lingering reverence –
how do I serve
this dead young man? –
love's an upending majesty,
love's a make-do
ladder to grief:
vehement pledges,
and green limbs, green limbs…

THE HUMMINGBIRD

Bright whirligig that knows no grief,
sudden gem whose engine
is diligent and beatific,
in pure communion,
I've opened and taken you
deep into my being.

Scion to your quick colors,
your tiny hosannas, I poise
before my love's body
become a thousand thimbles of weeping
for dawn,
keen galaxy I'd test and savor
with a deft, regaling bill:
all this majesty is for me –

Now the hours are deities
of nectar and sweat.
Now the hours are flower-gorged,
filled with his breath –

Suddenly, I'm flying
backward,
fleet hovering in the moment,
breakneck marionette:
grit gone, God yes,
and panic's balcony:
the carnage in the eye burned away.

LOVE POEM OF THE CRETAN SPRING

I.

I've found a place;
the door's loden green.
You'll be beguiled by
the perfumes of the garden.
Come be with me
in Greece,
and write your poems.
You love peace,
and I love peace –

You have an owl's gaze:
civetta,
I call you,
as you show me how to eat
a fresh wild rose.

You are leonine,
yet giving,
burly, tongue-tied
with strangers,
but eloquent
one on one,
at times fierce
as a beach torch
or a catamount's cry.

You are a page of Blake
blown open by the wind.

II.

I don't know what schedule suits
the roosters,
the good cockerels of Crete,
but from our happy,
disheveled bed,
we hear their blunt heralding,
their braggadocio,
far into the day.

III.

In a nearby bungalow,
always sweet commotion,
daily festival: a dance troupe
showers us with fleet
choreography and joy.

As the earth's face
grows serene,
under our windows,
alluring lemons,
a small boy savoring
tic-tac-toe
on a dusty flank
of the dazzling troupe's
dilapidated van.

IV.

And the beauty we glean
in the hills
as we journey
on deferring donkeys,
windmills spinning beside
our intimate jests
and silences,
is the glory of rocky breastplates,
unregenerate shields.

v.

Like island mountains,
antimacassared, shawled
with snow,
that in their aegis
seem to cherish
the faultless,
indefatigable sea,
so I've pondered and adored
your impeccable legs,
your curved, intrepid lips,
which have been
my fulfillment –

Drawing fresh water
near a cave church,
pregnant with cool psalms, icons,
suddenly I see,
on Crete and Santorini,
with you, I've become
all insouciance and praise,
vivacity and worship.

VI.

Now in a driftwood fortress
fronting the sea,
you glean a stray
gull feather, and begin
a deft stroking
of my limbs,
my nape;
I like this, I like
how easily your joy
and prowess become
invention, artful
man of the Giotto eyes:

at our juncture of earth
and purgative water,
dune and skin,
desire – voluminous,
          your brinesoaked hair
          brushing my throat;
desire – write it on my flesh,
          spell it in cool sand;
desire – the fugitive quill
          first an aphrodisiac
          fingertip and brow,
          then a beachside boutonniere.

VII.

Here comes the troupe
with a madcap
surfeit of glass plates;
porous with Metaxa,
with glistening sea,
everyone dances
among broomswept shards
with such whole,
heartfelt zest,
our figures seem to flicker
in and out of time –
like fireflies flung broadcast
by a gust,
or Queen Anne's lace
the sultry spring proffers:
bouquet of pure being, deluge
of *now, now, now.*

VIII.

We sleep in caves
at Matala.
Tommaso comes to visit,
and you alternate
carrying me up the hill
to the ruined palace
of Ayía Triáda –
first in your vying,
dallying arms,
then on your backs,
then balanced upon
your reliable shoulders,
in a kind of piquant competition,
mock appraising
my dangling legs,
making larkish offerings
of wildflowers –
cyclamen, anemone, crocus –
past olive pickers
with dark nets,
diligent, oblivious
to our lunacy;
from the double height,
I can see where
the vast sea shimmers toward
the ochres of Egypt.

IX.

We slip and tumble
down a slope of olives.
I feel the anodyne
of your beard, your lips,
where a bruise
darkens. The wind rises.
Tommaso, no longer visible,
laughs overhead.

Now, in a light, easeful rain,
you manacle my wrists
with kisses,
and we pour into each other
deep mirthful
draughts of flesh.

X.

May I have one, too – a kiss
from your American friend?
Tommo, we laugh,
where did YOU *spring from?*
Open your shirts, he commands,
and begins to tear
petals of wildflowers –

I suppose it wouldn't hurt
to give my cat-faced cousin
a kiss.

XI.

As Tommaso dozes,
like an undivided Adam,
you tell me
as pubescent boys
you clung together
in a bed of coats,
after your brother drowned;
in your aunt's baronial armoire
he licked your palms,
and covered your belly with blossoms
he found in a park –

XII.

Sea birds coalescing
with hoary stars,
the Aegean growing
evermore lucent,
as if dawn could occur
underwater,
despite wolf's hour:

I dreamed we witnessed this,
arm in arm,
the unremitting sea
encircling Crete,
one sweeping panorama,
one poignant display –
dolphins and plundered pearls
suddenly apparent.

THE DREAM OF THE MINOAN
PALACE OF KNOSSOS

I.

Today, in Hersonissos, I woke
with a vestige
of anointing hands
at my nape;
I dreamed of an ample wedding,
an enveloping love
in the Palace of Knossos:

perhaps this is the seed,
why taut Minoan men,
lithe bull-leapers
with slender waists,
have always set,
for my part,
a touchstone of male beauty.

II.

In the fortifying dream,
it was heralded:
a peerless union
was entering the palace;
as the paired young men,
the complementary lovers, passed
through jostling witnesses
into an immense labyrinth
of halls and lustral basins,
lilies like sweet hurrahs
were tossed at their feet,
their petals
tinctured with elation.

III

At Knossos,
still numinous, rife
with phantoms,
there are no garlands
to greet us,
as we stroll
through the West Court,
the Corridor of Processions,
no lionizing crowd –
only a witnessing cypress,
a stray grasshopper
on a stairstep,
only the livelong hills,
terraced, ancestral,
that tower above
any lovers,
in luxuriant spring,
on the Taurean, goat-trodden
island of Crete.

ARC

The wild sweet work of union:

you cover me,
as the engrossing sea,
the neighboring wind,
might cover me,
with the clearest insistence –

till, all at once, I recall,
from the Iráklion museum,
the blue dolphin fresco:
supple harbingers,
jesters –
how could I have guessed
they'd come
to suffuse me
with their freshness –

I feel your cool, unfaltering
fingers on my tongue,
an inchoate fire
in my spine, in each
atom of my body.

And I swear this time
we'll ascend to the place
where the Beloved reclaims us:

stopless, pellucid place –

Relinquishers,
bliss breathers,
illusionless, in Aegean air,

the dolphins arc above hazard.

BEAUTIFUL SIGNOR

All dreams of the soul
End in a beautiful man's or woman's body.

— YEATS, "THE PHASES OF THE MOON"

Whenever we wake,
still joined, enraptured –
at the window,
each clear night's finish
the black pulse of dominoes
dropping to land;

whenever we embrace,
haunted, upwelling,
I know
a reunion is taking place –

Hear me when I say
our love's not meant to be
an opiate:
helpmate,
you are the reachable mirror
that demands integrity,
that dares me to risk
the caravan back
to the apogee, the longed-for
arms of the Beloved –

Dusks of paperwhites,
dusks of jasmine,
intimate beyond belief

beautiful Signor

no dread of nakedness

beautiful Signor

my long ship,
my opulence,
my garland

beautiful Signor

extinguishing the beggar's tin,
the wind of longing

beautiful Signor

laving the ruined country,
the heart wedded to war

beautiful Signor

the kiln-blaze
in my body,
the turning heaven

beautiful Signor

you cover me with pollen

beautiful Signor

into your sweet mouth –

This is the taproot:
against all strictures,
desecrations,
I'll never renounce,
never relinquish
the first radiance, the first
moment you took my hand –

This is the endless wanderlust:
dervish,
yours is the April-upon-April love
that set me spinning even beyond
your eventful arms
toward the unsurpassed:

the one vast claiming heart,
the glimmering,
the beautiful and revealed Signor.

II

AMALGAM

Above rooftops, bell towers,
in the beatific
amphitheater at Taormina,
I brush my lips
to your ruffled, jovial
helmet of hair,
as if we'd passed
into the limitless
(the bygone and the future
burned away), and left
the blurred, the jagged,
the fly-by-night
far below,
like a jabbering beehouse –
our souls unburdened
by rippling, recurring
turquoise and laudable blue,
Etna's turbulent glory.

Hobo-light,
in the hands of freedom,
we relish
the delicate seesaw
between timelessness
and the time at hand,
like the *click*, *click*,

of your rapacious camera:
here, here is the overrunning
present in all its fulgence,
spring at its heady maximum.
This is the providential place,
the deadsure belvedere,
where marrying sea and air,
fertile land and fire
commingle.
This is the elected place –
suddenly I know with surety –
I want to merge with you
with the subtlest fanfare,
to forge a true amalgam,
vibrant, consummate –
not happy-ever-aftering,
but dedicated wills,
parallel branches lit
by the green, restoring
fire at the core of May –

We're alone now,
unbarred.
We bribed the careworn,
neverminding guard
to let us in
a half an hour
before opening.
As we walk among ancient tiers,
snapped columns,
and Scotch broom, I'm remembering
how we became ardent
celebrants of Klimt,

amid December's cold
brocades of black and bone,
inveterate boys
making rakish, empowering wings
in an acre of Viennese white –
near our frisking,
snow on a Medusa
of stone,
the Danube breaking
into harps of ice.

We improvised
a tiny Christmas
of tinsel and blueberry wine;
you covered my eyes,
a mimic blindfold.
Wait, you said.
Suddenly I felt
your intent fingertips,
your lips transmit
a treasure trove
shock of wine,
strong as death –
the last veil
to our union, the last
atom of resistance,
utterly extinguished:
live with me,
live with me –

Under an unimpeded blue,
beside the hills'
exuberant emerald,

I call your nearness
holy, your spark
sweet and staggering,
because,
on this emperor-is-naked earth,
poisoned, glittering
as hush money,
yes, in precincts of lewd gold,
you are my catalyst,
my key turner.
There are no edges
to our loving now –

As if you brought me
to this austere theater
to fill me
with the island's divinity;
the volcano, with its flourish
of snow,
seems to loom
within reach.
Not long ago, we trekked
through the cold
toward the lip
of the roaring crater,
like peregrines in rugged
passage to the unmastered.
Recalling that ice
and restless fire
from a distance,
how simply it returns to us:
the grayblooded morning
a river's margins lapsed,

filling our faltered car,
then our cowed heartbeats,
our urgent journey
through the flood,
brackish, impinging,
till in the foursquare hush,
the aftermath,
we were lovers assuming
the identity of fire,
reaching the undeluged streets,
the dry land,
undemolished, aligned
with the only power
that's lasting,
superabundant, attainable
in jeopardy and poise:
love's power –

Spurred by vernal sunlight,
and the memory
of a childhood nurse,
once a boy of fourteen
seized a hideaway corner
behind barbed wire,
and opened his prison clothes.
And as some acts brace us,
so I imagine that emboldened boy,
vigorous,
transfigured here beside us,
with a ring bearer's bloom.
My love,
may there always be

a guiltless touch
in the places of desecration –

Your cupped hands
I drink from,
regal, insistent,
your cradling,
penny-colored eyes
persuade me
wherever there's a lover's
solicitous gaze,
unscripted joy,
the Nazarene still walks
the wounded earth
in unwavering tenderness –
rumor of the Soul of Souls,
glimpse of the Beloved –
igniting blossom
after human blossom:
the sweeping bridegroom,
the shepherd with his crown
of birds –

Love: the girasol in bloom,
the snake unvenomed,
sacramental, pacific.

Love: all my Potemkin villages
unmasked –
your steadfast limbs,
your capable loins,
a ladder-climb,

a luxury,
a helix to God –

On this peaceful,
emancipating height,
let's bequeath the parched,
the bitter man,
our tandem beauty
as eleemosynary light,
as testimony –
this antagonist
in the mind's eye;
beside a bier,
we heard him weep
my son, my son,
but this was the indurate world
he dreamed of:
the Davids and Jonathans he branded
soulless, nefarious,
tamped at last
with winterkilled leaves –

But look, as ever,
we spat-upon lovers live,
pledged men.

In you, the foothold,
the firmament.

In you, in you,
altar bread, justice,
the attar of home –

My lanternlike love,
justborn, willing,
maverick no more,
now I give you my deepest name.

ABOUT THE AUTHOR

Cyrus Cassells's first book, *The Mud Actor*, was a 1982 National Poetry Series selection and a finalist for the Bay Area Book Reviewers Award. Named as one of the Best Books of 1994 by *Publishers Weekly*, his second volume *Soul Make a Path Through Shouting* was also awarded the Poetry Society of America's William Carlos Williams Award, and was a finalist for the Lenore Marshall Prize for outstanding book of the year. He has been a recipient of the Peter I.B. Lavan Younger Poet Award of the Academy of American Poets and a Lannan Literary Award, among other honors. He is a graduate of Stanford University and the Centro Fiorenza Italian Language School in Florence, has worked as a translator, film critic, and actor, and has taught, most recently at George Mason University in Fairfax, Virginia. From 1991 to 1997 he lived primarily in Florence and Rome. He is currently living in San Francisco.

BOOK DESIGN & composition by John D. Berry Design, using Adobe PageMaker 6.0 on a Macintosh IIVX and a Power 120. The type is ITC Galliard, designed by Matthew Carter in 1978. Galliard is based on the 16th-century French humanist typefaces of Robert Granjon, although it is not a direct revival. This version was digitized by Matthew Carter in 1992 for Carter & Cone Type Inc. *Printed by Malloy Lithographing.*